Poison Ivy

By Beverly Pearl

This book is dedicated to the three most important people
in my life, Stephan, Andre and Nicky

ISBN 978-1-4357-1386-4

Contents

Chapter 1

Poison Ivy

It had been too hot for too long. Dried up stubble of what had most recently passed for grass stabbed at Ivy's sandal-ed feet. Dust clung to the sweat on her generously exposed skin. The weeds in the field had fruited early, as if they knew it was their last chance. Even common garden weeds were stunted. Ivy was used to it by now, though the change had seemed to come suddenly.

The pile of damp books in her arms felt heavy. A light breeze cooled the back of her neck only for a moment, and she looked up. Overhead a hawk circled in the cloudless sky. Weren't hawks supposed to be good luck? She scanned the rolling horizon for a tiny patch of green on the near edge of a field which had once been a magnificent garden, and quickened her pace.

Ivy had lived on the farm all her life. She still remembered pulling rocks out of the soil every spring, down by the willows, but that was 10 years ago. Now the willows were gone. The stream was just a crack in the earth that ran with water only after a storm. Storms did not bring relief from heat or drought.

On reaching the old farm house where she and her mother still lived Ivy always felt lighter. She shuffled into the soft blue pastels of the living room and collapsed on a burgundy lazy-boy, arms still full of books.

The chair sprang into action.

"Mother! Why can't you remember to turn off your chair?"

Ivy's mother had sore back muscles, which the chair might help if she could stay put in it long enough. Otherwise it was just another living room chair- one which might cost almost a year's tuition in places where they still used money. When left on, the slightest weight set the rollers under the fabric in motion. This trick had already inspired every cat in the house to cut a wide path around the burgundy chair. Most of the time it was the only chair without a cat on it.

Ivy pressed the switch on the arm of the chair and its indifferent, internal masseuse halted.

"Sorry, dear", mother called from the kitchen. "When I'm distracted by a call I sometimes forget."

'...Sometimes...', thought Ivy with mild annoyance. But this was her 17th birthday and she wasn't about to make it any worse than it already was by getting mad.

Ivy's eyes rested on dusty-blue drapes and she let her mind wander. Why was she the only one who ever felt this way? Why was she the only teen in the world who felt isolated?

These days, the fad seemed to be to express one's unhappiness in order to look sensitive and therefore attractive. There was even a name for this: "emo". Ivy found most of the teens who pretended sensitivity to be very shallow. Ivy repressed a vague feeling that something was missing or wrong in her life and began to rewrite her day through daydreams.

'The handsome boy of her dreams sat alone on a park bench as Ivy strolled by, his wavy, ash-blond hair glistening in the sun. His green eyes followed her out of sight. On her way back from the Elmvale Library she realized that he had waited for her return. He caught her attention with witticisms he'd been thinking up to impress her. Then he invited her to sit down beside him. Feigning interest in her library books he moved his lanky body closer. . . '

It was no use. She'd seen the boy, all right. He sat on the bench looking as handsome as ever, with a bunch of cool-looking kids. He watched as she stumbled, not quite falling, and the library books flew out of her arms. The books splashed through a fountain that seemed to double as a bird bath, spilling its contents. The boy even knew her name, though she didn't know how. But this time her fantasy would not save her from disillusionment.

He called her "Poison Ivy".

Chapter 2

The Visitors

"Poison Ivy" was a nickname that Ivy had not heard since
the forests were lush with leaves. In those days Ivy had a
bad case of poison ivy. The look of the blisters all over her
body lasted an eternity and seemed to frighten her young
peers. Never mind that some of them got it too. They
weren't named "Ivy". She hated her nickname. It was an
insult offered by other children to one who never seemed to
fit in at the best of times. It was reminiscent of her
physical and social clumsiness, which they seemed to think
poisoned their games.

As a child, Ivy had retired into books and dreams.

When the climate started to change, farmers in her area
became nervous. The last five years were the worst.
During that time Ivy's protagonists moved away. Her
nickname left with the last of them.

The town was nearly deserted until the industrialists came.
It was all part of a world-survival plan that had come

9

almost too late. Anywhere that might sustain vegetation had to be returned to either its natural state or, where soil toxicity levels permitted, used for farmland. In some cases this involved leveling cities to make room for life-giving trees. Dust bowls such as Ivy's mother's former farm were sold, abandoned or rented for other purposes. Most farmers had panicked and sold out early. Now those who had hung on could get by on the rental income from industrialists. Food could be expensive and hard to come by.

No one was doing really well these days, wherever or however they lived, but the new social norms had been assimilated. Things were starting to settle down.

The change had been hard for Ivy too. She missed the green, the colourful flowers and abundant fruit. The one thing she liked was that it shook up the order. People were too busy adapting to changes in their own lives to call her names. None the less, on her 17th birthday the dreaded nickname had returned to destroy her favorite romantic dream.

"Happy birthday, dear."

Ivy's mother, Jane, stood over her with an enormous platter of little cakes.

"Thanks. I take it you'll be drying some of that for later," Ivy said, feigning enthusiasm.

She and her mother got on pretty well. Ivy didn't want to hurt her mother's feelings but predictable kindness from someone who was supposed to care anyway wasn't lifting her mood.

"Why don't you freshen up, Ivy, and we'll celebrate your birthday. I've invited the Johnsons to join us. They're new in town."

"New like everyone else," said Ivy.

Jane knew everyone because she owned most of the land considered suitable for building in the area... that is, land suitable for nothing else.

Ivy's father had panicked and fled to the city when farming real-estate plummeted but Jane sat tight with her only child. They never saw him again.

Later, as planned re-locations took place, the farm was slowly divided up to form the encroaching suburbs of Elmvale. Jane was one of the few independent land owners left in North America. Government-capped, subsidized rentals were low but with so much land to subdivide Jane could make a living. It helped the already overworked central government, too, if people were willing to manage their own land. Jane was every-one's first contact.

And now, as if it wasn't hot enough and dull enough on the worst birthday ever, Ivy also had to dress for a celebration with people she didn't even know. Reluctantly, Ivy put down her book and heaved herself out of the chair. Then her breath caught in her throat.

Through the front window, coming down the path toward her house, was the blond boy from the park who had called her "Poison Ivy". She watched, mouth open, as his exact replica stepped sullenly out of a red, Smart car parked in her driveway. An older woman who didn't look at all like the boys emerged last. She appeared to be herding the second boy along.

Ivy ran upstairs, feeling as if her life was over. Bravely she turned down her full-length mirror, prepared to primp for as long as it took. Astonished brown eyes stared back at her. Her black hair hung in limp clumps cut just above her shoulders and dirt from the day's walk still clung to her brown body. This would take work.

Mercifully, Jane had already laid Ivy's birthday present on the bed- a stylish, lemon-yellow, cotton top with denim-blue shorts. It was skimpy enough to wear in this weather and flattering to Ivy's boyish figure. Half an hour later she was stumbling down the stairs, hair not completely dry. She arrived breathless at the doorway to the living room, paused and swallowed hard before making an entrance.

The sullen boy's expression slowly morphed into amusement as his mother introduced the family.

"Ivy, meet David and Don. My husband, Tom, had to stop by the lab first, and I'm Isla."

Isla was Native Canadian, like Ivy. This family was from the former City of Kirkland Lake. They were relocated when that city had to be leveled for eventual rehabilitation as a tropical fruit farm. Now Isla and Tom worked at the soil purification research lab in West Elmvale.

Don and David were identical twins but it wasn't hard to tell which one Ivy had seen in the park.

"Well, if it isn't Poison Ivy," Don grinned.

Chapter 3

The Present

Ivy brushed an orange cat off the blue rocking chair as Isla shot a disapproving glance at Don. Out of the corner of her eye she saw David watching for her reaction and decided to give him none.

She longed to curl up in the rocking chair with a book, without all these people around. She fixed her gaze on Isla.

"How long have you been in Elmvale?" Ivy asked politely, trying to make conversation.

David's expression became blank and Don affected an air of irritated boredom.

"We've been here almost a month now. Your mother helped us to get settled and has been showing my husband and I around."

Just then Jane appeared in the door with the tray of cakes. Trust Mother to diffuse an uncomfortable situation.

"Ivy, why don't you show the boys the garden while Isla and I chat."

Ivy stumbled to her feet. The boys followed, grabbing

as many cakes as they could carry as they passed the tray.

The late afternoon air had already started to cool things down. How stuffy the living room was by comparison at this time of day. There was something about being in that lush little patch of garden that lifted the spirits.

"Don't you even want to know where I found out your nickname?" Don blurted.

"Now that you mention it..." Ivy began.

"No, Don," David cut in. "That is, not until we give her the birthday present."

David reached into his pocket and drew out a legal-sized envelope folded around a small, white, rumpled package. Eagerly, he pushed it into Ivy's hand.

The envelope contained a map penciled on to note paper. The parcel, no bigger than a walnut, had been hastily wrapped in tissue and secured with string. It contained a key.

"Aren't we a little old for treasure hunts?" asked Ivy, affecting an air of 'cool'.

"It's on your property," said David. "That means that if there is something there it must belong to you."

It was true. Ivy's family had been on the farm for generations, but how would these strangers from the north know that? Her tone became serious.

"Where did you get this?"

David put out his hand as if to stop Don from speaking.

"To be honest, we never did get her name. A woman wearing way too much costume jewelery gave it to us at the train station just before we left for Elmvale.

Don smirked at David's description of the woman. David's expression never changed.

"She said to give it to you and to no one else. We thought you would know what it was all about," David continued.

Ivy screwed up her face as she tried to imagine anyone in her family who might fit that description.

"Anyway," Dave continued, "I think we owe it to ourselves to try to follow the map."

"Spoken like a true bookworm-sleuth," Don responded.

Don moved closer to Ivy.

"The woman said that they used to call you 'Poison Ivy'."

Ivy blushed. By now she didn't really trust Don but Dave seemed reasonable enough, and they were both identically cute.

She turned to Dave.

"I've never seen identical twins act so different," she said.

"We get that a lot," Don cut in. Still speaking to Dave, Ivy continued,

"Have you ever been here before?"

"No," Dave responded. "We asked around and none of the other kids seemed to know you. The librarian pointed you out last week. Then we had to be sure that you were the right 'Ivy'. Don figured that out when he made you drop your books in the birdbath."

Ivy blushed again.

"Is that why you came here?"

"No", the boys responded simultaneously.

This time Don spoke.

"We didn't know you'd be here. It was a social obligation. If I wanted to use the car tomorrow I'd have to attend some girl's birthday today...turned out to be you."

"And we're glad we came," added Dave, attempting to save the moment. "Happy birthday."

It was too weird. Ivy WAS intrigued, but growing weary of this game.

A long evening stretched ahead. It seemed that she could spend it either eating cake in her living room with two reluctant guests or strolling around the property with these strange, young men.

"OK. Let's follow the map and see where it leads us," she responded.

Chapter 4

Mystery Woman

The map was hard to read after three weeks in a pocket. Ivy, Don and Dave huddled together on the back deck, unaware that a tray of cakes and tea had appeared on the table behind them.

Suddenly a deep male voice broke the silence.

"That must be pretty important!"

The three jumped guiltily and then, realizing that they had done nothing wrong, just as quickly regained composure.

Except for a shock of salt and pepper hair that he kept brushing out of his eyes the man appeared to be an older version of David and Don,

Isla and Jane laughed and introduced Tom, the boys' father. Now the party was complete and the map would have to wait.

"We thought we could all have snacks on the back deck where it's cooler."

Like two bookends, Dave and Don leaned in opposite

directions against the porch, faces impassive. Ivy sat primly on the edge of the glider, ready to balance a tea cup for as long as she had to.

"Do we have any relatives who wear too much jewelery?" she asked.

Isla answered, directing her response to Jane.

"The boys must have told Ivy about the mystery woman who approached them at the train station. I meant to ask you who you know from Kirkland Lake."

"We don't know anyone from Kirkland Lake but the way people move around these days one never knows from which direction they will come," Jane responded.

Isla continued, "She was waiting by the train bound for Elmvale. ...looked Cree, if you ask me... about 50 years old, though you can never tell... and she did wear lots of jewelery... Seemed to know all about Ivy and was very insistent that the boys find her."

A look of puzzlement and concern crossed Jane's face.

"Oh, she seemed harmless enough," Isla continued. "She introduced herself as an old family friend of yours."

Ivy's hand moved toward the note in her pocket but Dave stopped her with his eyes.

The boys shuffled over and took their places on either side of Ivy, cakes in hand.

"Ixnay for the time being," Don whispered in her ear, on his way to assuming his customary sprawl against the back of the glider.

What an unusual day this had turned out to be. It was like living a novel. Through a haze of idle conversation Ivy watched the shadows in the garden lengthen. She felt content in the presence of two strange, new friends who flanked her on the swing. She wished there had been more time to decipher the map.

The evening ended abruptly. After an eternity of conversation about water purification breakthroughs Isla and Tom stood up simultaneously and began a seemingly endless round of thank-you's. This was Dave and Don's cue to do the same, which they did with considerably less fanfare. As he slid into the car Don turned to wink at Ivy... and they were gone.

In her pocket, her fingers rested on a crumpled map and a key.

Chapter 5

The Storm

Ivy awoke with the unrelenting ring of a telephone intruding on some dream. Jane was already out in the garden.

The ringing persisted as Ivy groped sleepily in a pile of pastel blue and pink pillows, pushed off the bed during a restless sleep. Finding the phone at last, she allowed her body to slide off rough, bamboo-fiber sheets onto the cool floor.

A soft cave of pillows engulfed her as the nagging ring ceased and she sighed a sleepy greeting into the phone.

"Ivy! Did I wake you?"

It was Don- or Dave. She couldn't tell their voices apart yet though mannerisms made it easy to see which was which.

Ivy sat up, suddenly alert.

"Have you figured out the map yet?"

Now she knew it must be Don.

Ivy reached for a pair of shorts that sprawled on the floor. It was still there, safely in one pocket.

"No. Still trying," she responded.

Ivy swallowed hard.

"Want to help?"

"Dave has a few chores and I have a make up test to do over the Internet. Maybe we could come this afternoon. Do you have enough shovels?"

"Yes. I might not have it all figured out by then. You saw the condition that map was in. But you're welcome to come and help."

Ivy's day had suddenly become complicated. She didn't know whether to feel elated or suffocated. A morning just musing over the events of the night before, while going about her chores, would have been within her comfort zone. Now her secret love who had turned into two imposing people compelled her to snap to awareness and focus on possibilities.

She examined the map. There was no indication of North- only an "X" for the house and an "X" to mark the spot. Landmarks were few and smudged. With some thought she was able to narrow it down to the north or west side of the property, depending on whether a blurred mass was meant to be a rocky outcrop or a forest, now extinct. The stream cut a diagonal path in front of the rock face and through the forest. She decided to try the forest first. Then she pulled on her old coveralls and hurried about her chores.

Ivy's work around the the garden was minimal because she sometimes puttered among the brittle plants, pulling only the inedible weeds just for pleasure. Today two of the solar dehydrators were ready to be emptied into jars. The dry rain barrels that fed the garden through a soaker hose didn't need much cleaning. The last reservoir held only a foot of water but at least sand hadn't blown in.

She tried to study the sky, but there was nothing to study. The air held so little moisture that it was almost a uniform blue. There was not even a breeze. No matter. Storms seemed to blow up out of nowhere these days. The longest the rain barrels had been completely dry this summer was two weeks.

A voice broke into her thoughts.

"All finished your chores?"

Ivy whirled around to face Don.

"Sorry to scare you. Do you have the shovels? Dave will come later but we can get started."

Suddenly Ivy wasn't thinking about chores. She reached into the pocket of her overalls for the map and started to explain its possibilities.

"I think we should check the other side of the forest first," she said, pointing more decisively than she felt. "The shovels are in the shed, which is on the way."

Don squinted as if to try to make sense of a tangle of gleaming, white bramble in the distance, shrugged and followed Ivy down the path to the shed.

"You can use your shovel as a walking stick," Ivy instructed, pushing a shovel at Don. "And stay on the path. It's easy to sprain an ankle in there.

The forest on Ivy's property was a 10 minute walk from the shed. It was one of the few left in the area that hadn't been completely destroyed by fire. Lightening strikes were so common during electrical storms that even small houses were required by law to have a substantial lightening rod. Windmills that stretched almost out of site into the sky were scattered throughout the community because that made it less likely for them to all be damaged at once by a storm. It was all about decentralization these days, and making do.

Don prattled cheerfully as they trudged down the path, shovels clinking behind them.

He told Ivy that both of his parents were engineers. Back in Kirkland Lake Don's mother had developed a battery that could be connected to a lightening rod to harness the intense electrical energy of a lightening strike. A few experimental houses had these batteries connected to their rods. The technology was there. It was just too expensive and inefficient to be wide spread.

Suddenly the landscape changed.

It was like trudging through a graveyard. All along the path ghosts of trees lay toppled, broken, tangled in an eerie mass for as far as the eye could see. These once proud sentries now leaned precariously against one another, barkless and bleached by the sun.

"I didn't realize..."

Don's voice trailed off.

"This part was mostly white pines," said Ivy.

Then they fell silent.

The sun's intensity increased as shadows shortened. Clouds of dust billowed with every footstep and stuck to their sweat. Ivy insisted on following the path even though they could see its twists and turns into the distance over the rubble of a levelled forest.

At last they stopped where an old, cracked stream bed cut the path dividing the bones of the forest in two. It was a deep gouge in the earth that extended out of sight in both directions. A few remnants of willow root still stuck out from its crumbling sides.

Ivy threw down her shovel and turned away from Don

to hide her humiliation.

"If it was buried here, it was washed away long ago," she grumbled. "The only landmark the map could have been pointing to at this place was a big willow tree."

"Don't come here often?" Don replied.

"I'm not allowed. The forest and the stream are considered too dangerous," she replied, embarrassed at sounding like a kid.

As if to rub it in, Don slid down the 6- foot bank into the cracked stream bed and extended his arms lavishly. Ivy scowled and looked into the distance.

Her body tensed.

"Get out of there!" Ivy yelled.

Don smirked and scuffed the cracked and hardened clay with his sandal.

"I mean it! Get out! Get out now!" screamed Ivy, pointing to the horizon.

A slight breeze moved her hair as low, ominous rumble muffled the echo of her voice. A tiny strip of dark gray lay like a ribbon across the horizon. Alarmed by her intensity but trying to appear cavallier, Don tried to climb out. Loose gravel broke away sending him back. The rumble was growing louder. The air became heavy. This time, he felt the urgency. He ran at the side, arms extended toward her outstretched hands. With both hands and the weight of her body Ivy pulled him off balance, over the edge and out of danger. He tumbled to the ground on top of Ivy. By now the rumble had become a roar. Don raised his head just in time to watch a wall of water rush down the gorge. In seconds the stream was a raging torrent.

Stunned, Don struggled to his feet. He turned to help

Ivy but she was already standing, grabbing his hand, running- in the wrong direction. The wind picked up. The ribbon was now a wall of gray on the horizon. Don heard himself shout over the roar of wind and water.

"Shouldn't we go back?"

"We'll never make it!" Ivy shouted back. "Our only hope is to get behind those rocks!"

A small, rocky outcrop 10 meters away still gleamed in the sun behind a haze of streaming dust. This time when they ran Don was pulling Ivy along, faster than she could go. The sky went black. A deluge of rain stung their skin like bullets as they slipped through the muck, stumbling over dried branches and roots. Moments later they huddled together on the lee side of a large boulder to wait out the storm.

And it was over as quickly as it began.

Chapter 6

The Journey Home

The sky was suddenly bright. Beads of water glistened on dry soil. Cracks, damp from rivulets, were already drying up. A light mist rose from the parched earth. Ivy could feel the mud start to tighten on her skin. She felt Don's body close to hers, felt his grip loosen to a caress, felt the softness of his cheek against hers. She was afraid to look at Don.

"Ivy?"

"It's over, Don."

Reluctantly they released one another from what had begun as a fearful embrace. There was no hurry now.

Grasping their protective boulder, they pulled themselves to their feet. Ivy glanced timidly at Don's astonished face. Then, forgetting their pride, they both burst into laughter.

Except for the parts of their bodies protected by the embrace, they were completely coated with muck.

"We look as ghastly as the trees!" Ivy exclaimed.

This time they were not running as they crunched through

the fallen branches and rocks that led back to the path. A feeling of calm camaraderie tuned their footsteps to one-another. To speak would be to break the spell. No one spoke. As they approached the path the rhythmic pat of their footsteps slowed in unison. Don touched Ivy's shoulder.

"I like you, Ivy."

Ivy's heart was in her throat. She hadn't bothered to shake the mud out of her hair or rub it off her face and arms. She remembered when mud was tried to cure her poison ivy and how a neighbor had joked that she looked like a mud monster. Don looked pretty interesting too as he stood there grinning, his hair spiked and disheveled with muck flaking off. It kind of leveled the playing field.

Ivy smiled back.

"I like you too."

When they reached the forest path the stream bed was already dry. One of the shovels had been swept downstream. Don picked up the other and stabbed at the ground. Under a thin layer of muck it was bone dry.

"With all that mud, you'd think the rain would soften the ground!" he complained.

He joined Ivy on the path.

"Will your mum be angry that we lost a shovel?"

"Probably. It could be sticking out of the mud some-where. We'll find it later. If we're lucky it was swept down-stream far enough to be caught by the Intake's grid."

"The Intake" was a plant designed to collect and purify precious water from the stream when storms came. By now there would be a work crew at the grid that framed the entrance to the plant, clearing debris. Not long ago the grid had collected the body of an unfortunate child who had been surprised by the suddenness of the torrent. As a result, closer to town the banks of the stream were being reinforced and fences erected.

Don shuddered.

"You know, it's hard to get used to all the brown," he said, changing the subject. "In Kirkland Lake it was always green. *What* was green changed- I mean... We went from dying pine trees to struggling palm trees over about a ten year period. Some of us thought it was an improvement. But unless you are a farmer you're not even allowed to live there!"

Ivy said only, "You get used to it."

By the time they reached the shed the sun was high overhead.

"It must be noon. There are chores I'm supposed to do when a storm is coming and after it's gone," Ivy continued.

Then she remembered that she'd fortuitously forgotten to replace the lids on the rain barrels. All she had to do was cover them again.

Real life was seeping back in. Mud turned back to concrete as they trudged through the heat. Fresh dust clung to the sweat on their skin, even on the clean side. The magic was gone. Don felt it too.

"I guess the map is ruined now," he challenged.

Ivy felt in her pocket, on the clean side.

"It was on the side that was pressed against you," she countered. "We can try the rock face later."

Chapter 7

The Rock Face

Jane waited out the storm at the Johnson's house. Part of her job as a land-owner was to see that newcomers adapted to their new environment. When a strip of gray appeared on the horizon she had hurried right over. While Isla and Tom gaped at the deluge through the triple-pained windows of a fortress built to house researchers at work, Jane made sure that Dave collected precious water at home. As soon as the storm ended they re-covered the rain barrels.

Then Dave returned to Jane's house to meet Don and Ivy.

Don was replacing the last lid on a rain barrel as Dave stepped on to the back deck. Ivy was tying up battered plants in the garden. She stood up in time to see Dave and his almost unrecognizable replica walking toward her. For the first time since the adventure began, it occurred to her that Jane might want some answers.

"Look at you guys," Dave teased. "I can't leave you alone for a moment."

He winked at Ivy.

"We'll have to clean him up before Mum and Dad get back," said Dave.

Ivy felt a clump of hair, thick with clay, bump against her shoulder. This wasn't going to be easy.

"We may have to tell my mum about the map, now," she offered.

"Where's your imagination?" said Don, recovering his old arrogance. "We went for a walk and got caught in the rain."

"And the shovel?"

"Let's try to find it first."

Dave shot an irritated look at Don and said,

"We've been invited for lunch. Is there anywhere you two could sneak off to and clean up?"

But their concerns were misplaced. Jane had already hung two towels and two bathrobes over the railing on the back porch. As usual Jane was doing what she could to keep Ivy's dignity intact. Ivy had few enough friends and Jane worried.

Sometime when they were comfortable together Ivy would tell Jane all about her adventure with Don, embellishing just enough to present herself as a credible hero. For now all she could think of was how good it would be to be clean and fed.

Lunch was a more hurried affair than a morning like that deserved. Even so, it was already 2:00 when they set out on their second journey. For a change Dave was the one trying to rush things. Had Don shown more enthusiasm for this afternoon excursion Ivy might have thought that there were things the boys weren't telling her. Why should *they* care so much about something they might find in a hole on her property?

Jane made them all snacks to take along, wrapped in edible packaging. She gave them each a water belt with at least two bottles of water. She insisted that all three wear special, white, sun-blocking capes that reached to their calves and broad, white hats. Despite protection afforded by the mud Don's fair skin wouldn't take much more. When they put on their sunglasses Jane insisted on taking their picture.

Then, looking like three bizarre spies in a B-grade movie the adventurers set out for the rock face. This time it was just a scouting mission. They wouldn't take shovels. They would check the landscape against the map and maybe scout the stream for the missing shovel. If they found it Jane wouldn't have to know it had been lost.

The rock face was a wide slab of pink granite set in a weathered hillside. It slanted up and away from the farm, ending abruptly in a cliff. It's precipice was only 4 meters from the sloping ground below but the overall slope of the land was enough to obscure the view from Ivy's bedroom window all the way to the road. Ivy wondered why anyone would hide something where it was protected from the house but vulnerable to any passer-by.

"If we walk up the rock we'll have a view. From there we can see if it matches the map," Dave suggested.

This time Dave led the way. The slab of granite felt steeper than it looked as it crept up the hillside. It grew steeper as it stubbornly left the weathered hill behind. Still, the view from the top seemed disappointing.

"We could have seen almost as much from under the cliff

and not got so hot!" Don complained.

There was no shade. The rock was still too hot to sit on so Ivy spread her cape on the ledge.

"These things have good insulating value," she said.

"You wouldn't know it from wearing one in this heat," Don replied.

He removed a water bottle from his belt and sipped the warm water. Ivy laid the map out and oriented it to the scene that stretched before them.

"This is it!" Ivy exclaimed excitedly. "This mark here is that rock and there is the stream, and..."

It was unmistakable. From where they stood on the cliff all the landmarks matched up.

"If this map is accurate we should start digging right over there", she said, pointing to a spot beside the stream bed.

Suddenly they forgot how hot they were. They forgot the missing shovel. All that mattered was getting to the spot where the treasure was buried. The three fairly ran back down the rock, over the edge and down to the stream bed.

"It looks different from here," said Don, as he ran toward the stream bed.

Then they stopped short.

"I think the spot was around there," said Ivy, pointing to the edge of the stream.

Don looked nervously at the horizon.

"Well, we don't have the shovels with us anyway," he said wearily.

"We can eat our lunch over there," Dave added, gesturing toward the rock face.

By four in the afternoon the cliff afforded some protection from the sun if you sat right under it on the slightly convex, Western edge. From there you could see where the eastern edge of the rock jutted belligerently into the stream bed. Straight ahead, along a gradual, northern slope, a bank of lofty windmills turned slowly in breezes that never touched the earth.

Three teens collapsed against the cliff and opened their water bottles.

"If you sit still you might feel some breeze at this time of day," Ivy sighed.

They lounged against the cliff and started rustling through their snacks- cakes left over from Ivy's birthday.

"Maybe we should look for the shovel tomorrow," Don mumbled over an overfull mouth.

But Dave was starting to feel energized by the snacks.

"Is there a shortcut to the forest?" he asked, ignoring Don's thinly veiled complaint.

This time Ivy scanned the horizon before pointing to a place where the stream disappeared behind rock.

"Then let's get going. We'll need the shovels tomorrow for sure and we can't risk having Ivy get in trouble," he added.

"Thank you, I think," Ivy responded, clamoring to her feet.

It seemed cool to acknowledge a possible undertone of concern for themselves. But David, already well on his way, did not notice and Don was in no mood for humor.

When Ivy reached the bank Dave was already standing in the stream bed. Don scanned the horizon and quickened his step as Ivy ducked below the crevice to join Dave.

He arrived, breathless and lay on his belly to peer in. Ivy and Dave were examining something not easily seen from above. Two meters down, wedged in the clay where bank met stream-bed, an object glinted in the sun.

Ivy stood up suddenly. Her hair brushed Don's cheek on the edge of the bank as she tossed it back. Then she peered into his face with wide-eyed excitement and blurted the obvious,

"There's something sticking out of the bank. It must have been uncovered by erosion."

Chapter 8

Ghosts

Don's look softened to something that reminded Ivy of their adventure in the forest.

"Let me help you out of there."

Dave cleared his throat. He held out his cupped hands to offer her a boost. Smiling, Don pulled her up into his arms. Then they turned to help Dave over the bank.

"We can find the shovel today and investigate the object tomorrow," Dave said. "That thing is too well stuck to be going anywhere fast, anyway."

The three set out along the bank. Within minutes they reached the steep, narrow slash in the earth where rock met clay.

"This is the short cut," said Ivy.

This time they all scanned the horizon and listened carefully before moving on. A storm anywhere upstream could turn this part of the stream bed into a death trap. They scrambled down the bank and followed the bed deep into a canyon. Here the channel narrowed and curved around the edge of the rock face. On one side a rocky overhang towered above them. On the other was a steep, slippery cliff of clay. From down in the shadows everything looked bigger. The only way out was over an edge somewhere at either end of the canyon. Despite the heat they started running.

The gorge grew more narrow and deep with every footstep. Don took Ivy's hand and pulled to speed her up. Just ahead, Dave stopped to peer around the rock.

"We're only half way!" he shouted as they approached.

Dave grabbed Ivy's other hand. The boys fairly dragged her over the pebbled surface, as though running for their lives from a wall of water. At last the stream bed widened. The clatter of their footsteps became a soft thud as rock gave way to clay. They paused to catch their breath. A few roots sticking through the sides of the bank told them they had arrived at the beginning of the forest. Don reminded them that they were no safer if they stayed in this part of the stream bed. Able at last to leave it, the boys scrambled up the banks dragging Ivy with them.

"Next time we take the long way around," Don panted. He collapsed on to his cape, raising a puff of dust.

"We'll rest here a while and then look along the banks for the shovel," Dave wheezed unenthusiastically.

Ivy propped her cape on some whitened branches to create a shelter from the intense, late afternoon sun. Don drank some water and poured the last of it over his head. It was at least half an hour's walk home and they couldn't know how long it would take to find the spade, if they found it. Then Ivy asked a question which had bothered her from the beginning.

"Why is it so important to keep this a secret?"

Dave took a deep breath and let it out slowly.

"We have reason to believe that whatever is buried on your property may have broader implications than just some family heirloom. It may involve the government."

"What he means," said Don, "is that if we tell people someone else might get there first."

"...And I think it might be that object we saw sticking out of the stream bed, today. Think about it! That creek erodes every time a storm blows up. The banks are not where they used to be," Dave added.

"Why do you think the government would be interested?" Ivy asked.

"Because he likes to read mystery books," Don quipped as he sidled closer to Ivy.

This irritated David.

"It's more than that and you know it!"

The sharp tone left his voice as he spoke to Ivy.

"All in good time."

Now it was Ivy's turn to be irritated.

"The shadows are getting longer. We have to be back before dark. My water is all finished and I don't have time for these games. Let's find the shovel, or just go home!"

Ivy pulled up her makeshift tent and threw it around her shoulders. Donning her floppy, white hat and sunglasses she strode off toward the bank. The boys followed. Everyone was irritable in that heat. Dave touched her shoulder with his water bottle.

"Ivy? Have my water."

For a long time the only sound was the crunching of their footsteps.

Finally Don broke the silence.

"There's the path. The shovel has to be downstream from here. We'll find it. If you want to go home..."

"No. Actually, I've been enjoying this for the most part," Ivy interrupted. "We still have a few hours before dark. The worst that can happen is that *I'll* walk *you* home."

Don threw an arm around her and gave her a squeeze.

"You've never been to our house before, have you? If we haven't found the shovel by the time we get there at least you can have dinner. I'll drive you back."

"You can call you mother from our house," added Dave.

After that Ivy completely lost track of time. Don talked about his life in Kirkland Lake. He told her how much he missed the scented air, but not the humidity. He wished on-line study wasn't the best way to finish your education these days, because it's easier to charm the teachers in person. He joked about strange gizmos his parents developed in the name of progress, while everyone scrambled like ants to rebuild society.

Ivy and Don forgot to look for the shovel but Dave found it somewhere along the stream. She didn't remember leaving the forest behind- didn't notice when they left the bank to follow a path into town. She just found herself at the top of a familiar rise looking into the village that used to be part of Jane's farm. Don put his arm over her shoulder and pointed to a modern, adobe cottage on the edge of town. They set out toward it, with Dave leading the way.

As they approached the cottage, Don brightened. A pretty, blond girl dressed in pink was running up the path toward them. Dave glanced back at Ivy. Don just grinned.

"What time is it? I was supposed to meet Sandy after supper," said Don.

"Who's Sandy?" Ivy asked. She'd forgotten that in town Don always seemed to be surrounded by a group of kids.

"Don's girlfriend," Dave answered.

Trying to hide her disappointment, Ivy asked,

"Is she from around here?"

"I don't know. I've never heard of her," Dave responded dryly.

"Then how do you know she's his girlfriend?"

"Because they're all his girlfriend."

Despite his obvious discomfort, Don managed to save face.

"We're supposed to do homework together. I'm surprised she even recognized me in this get-up."

Sandy bounced toward them, her long, strawberry curls bobbing. She took a moment to decide which of the boys was Don and introduced herself to Dave. Then she turned to Ivy.

"Aren't you the girl who dropped her books in the fountain... the one they call Poison Ivy?"

Ivy flushed. She felt hurt, betrayed, trapped by a ghost.

This time it was Dave's hand she felt on her shoulder, turning her toward the cottage. Stunned and feeling out of place, she let herself be herded along with the effervescent Sandy.

Chapter 9

The Messenger

Sandy turned out to be much kinder than the little, blond girls Ivy remembered, and she was interesting. She seemed to know a little about everything. She was good to have along because she talked a lot, which meant that Ivy didn't have to. Dinner wasn't until 6 and that gave everyone plenty of time to find out that Sandy had studied dancing on the East coast and was trying to win a scholarship. Eventually she wanted to be a biologist, developing durable plant species with short growing seasons. She was sophisticated, smart and clearly enamored of Don. Ivy tried in vain to imagine Sandy's frail, perfect body climbing over rocks, covered in muck.

When the boys went off to help Tom set up some trays, Sandy turned her wide, blue eyes to Ivy.

"I got the impression that you don't like your old nickname. I've been meaning to apologize all night but I didn't want to bring it up again in front of the boys. Please accept my apology."

Ivy responded with irritation.

"Would you like to be called 'poison'?"

"No, I guess I wouldn't. I wasn't thinking. I hope we can be friends."

This girl was somehow too perfect.

"Sure," said Ivy.

"I told Don I'd help him with some homework after dinner. Maybe we can get together sometime?"

Ivy felt her appetite return. Before she could answer, Isla and the boys appeared with trays of vegetable canopies and a casserole.

This was not like any meal Ivy had ever experienced. Everyone talked at once, ate at once, got up and moved around. It was like a party. Sandy played her role as social lubricant brilliantly. Dave remained aloof and Don was... Don. Everyone ate a lot... except Sandy, and everyone had a good time. Then, like a storm, it was suddenly over. Isla and Tom went for a walk. Don and Sandy retired to Don's room to study together and for the first time Ivy was left alone with Dave.

Inspired by Sandy's performance, she tried to begin a conversation.

"What kind of books do you like to read?"

"Like Don said, I'm into mysteries," Dave responded. "But Ivy, you don't have to entertain me."

Seeing that his remark deflated her Dave continued.

"Do you like mysteries?"

"I suppose I might if I ever read them. I'm into Sci Fi... and you don't have to entertain me either."

They both laughed.

"If I was less tired I would consider asking you to go for a walk with me," said Dave. "Why don't we sit on the deck?"

"This is my favorite time of evening, because it's cool," Ivy blurted as they stepped outside.

She slouched on the glider, stretching her legs. Dave settled beside her.

"Now would be as good a time as any to tell you what this is all about," he said.

"I'm listening."

"I'll tell everything I've heard and you have to remember that it's only hearsay."

"Sure," she drawled sleepily.

Despite his flair for the mysterious, Ivy trusted Dave.

"The woman at the train station said she knew your father."

Ivy started and sat bolt upright.

"Sit back, Ivy. I knew this wouldn't be easy."

Ivy hadn't seen her father since she was 8 years old. Their once prosperous farm had just produced disastrous yields. Mother and father started talking in whispers. Jane looked worried all the time. Then her father just disappeared. Jane said he'd left to make his fortune and planned to return the conquering hero. He never returned. Eventually both Ivy and Jane had stopped watching the end of the driveway.

"You mean, he's alive?"

Dave continued.

"I haven't seen him. I don't know. Rumor has it that he got into trouble somewhere and just kept going. The woman with the map said she'd been hanging around the train station for days. She said she was looking for a messenger. Her instructions were to find some preppy-looking teenagers on their way to Elmvale. Your nickname was a kind of code- a way for the teen agers to be sure it was you."

By now Ivy was clutching Dave's arm.

"Well, why didn't he just contact my mum?" she exclaimed.

"I asked the same thing. It gets worse. Are you ready for this?

"He didn't exactly leave on good terms. He wanted to take Jane and you with him. When Jane refused to leave the farm he struck out on his own. He knew he was abandoning you at a difficult time. He also knew that Jane was a smart woman and wouldn't let anything happen to you."

It sounded so cliched.

"You don't have to protect me, Dave. It's been nine years. I hardly remember him."

He cleared his throat and began again,

"At first he was just a drifter like everyone else. Then he got caught stealing, like everyone else. The prisons were already full of drifters, so they let him off. Finally he met this woman- the one I met at the train station. They drifted together for a while and then settled as hands on a coconut farm in Kirkland Lake. I don't think he wants to have to face Jane."

"So, how does the map come in?" Ivy asked.

Well, it seems that a year or so after he left, he snuck back at night and buried something on your property. I think the river is about to uncover it."

Ivy closed her eyes and slumped back against his arm, resting on the back of the glider. Her father had returned. He returned and didn't even come to see her.

"So, you're the messenger."

Dave sat back too.

"I don't like spreading rumors. What we find in the box determines what we tell Jane, and how."

There was nothing left to say.

The slamming of the front door signaled Tom and Isla's return. From Don's open window Sandy's giggle rippled through the night air.

Dave and Ivy swayed peacefully on the glider, letting it all sink in.

Chapter 10

Treasure

He stood in a lush, grassy field, tall and handsome- Dave, or Don- it didn't matter. Ivy's hair swished across his body as she whirled in circles around him, twisting, writhing, heart pounding, hot... Still dancing, her body lost control, engulfed by rhythmic waves of passion and pleasure. All tension melted and Ivy woke with a sigh.

The sun was already at 10:00. Dave had suggested getting an early start to avoid the noon-day sun. ...Too late for that now. After a day like yesterday the boys probably slept in too.

Ivy dressed quickly. She filled some water bottles and stuffed her pockets with crackers on the way out. There was no one in sight, not even Jane.

"Must have gone into town," she heard herself say.

The phone was ringing. Ivy ran back inside. She caught it on the fifth ring.

A sweet, feminine voice on the other end said,

"Ivy? It's Sandy."

Ivy sighed and sat down.

"This isn't the best time. I have to go somewhere today."

"Well, I have four tickets to the theater tonight. I thought we might all go- you, Dave, Don and me."

"Can I call you back? I don't know how long this will take."

Soft lips touched her ear with a light kiss. A voice whispered,

"Say yes."

. . . and she jerked around to face Don.

"Yes," she said without thinking, and then into the receiver, "Yes, I'll go."

Dave was standing in the door with two shovels.

"C'm'on sleeping beauty."

The boys *had* slept in, but they brought the car. This time they were all outfitted, except for the spy suits which Ivy supplied. This time the troupe strode purposefully to the edge of the stream under the lip of the rock face. They took turns, alternately watching the sky and hacking at the unrelenting earth around the object. It was harder work than any of them expected. By lunch time a large, silver-coloured suit case had started to emerge.

Ivy felt in her pocket for the key that she'd pinned into her shorts the night before.

When at last they dragged a heavy, metal suit case from its tomb the sun was at 2:00. Sweaty and exhausted, the boys pushed it up over the bank while Ivy pulled. Then they helped each other out of the stream bed. They dragged the case to the rock face, collapsing at last into a shaded area that had started to expand along the edge.

The moment had arrived. Ivy's fingers trembled as she

released her key from its pin. She dug some dirt out of the lock. The key fit perfectly but it wouldn't turn.

"There's probably more dirt stuck in it. Blow in it," Don advised.

They blew in it, shook it and kicked it. Ivy tried the key again. It turned but the box wouldn't open.

"Probably rusted," said Don.

He kicked the case against the rock and it opened, spilling its contents.

For a moment no one said anything. Then Don said,

"At least we know what's in it."

"Now we know what it feels like to dig up confederate money," said Dave.

Ivy searched through the bills for a note or some news of her father.

"They still use money some places," she countered. "Even here it comes in handy sometimes."

"Yes, but I can't help thinking how valuable this cash was when it was buried and how much things have changed since then," Dave concluded. "There has to be $50,000.00 here."

"And I can't help wondering what we'll tell my mum," Ivy added, remembering her conversation with Dave the night before. "He was hiding it from us."

"Now that we know it, why not tell her the truth?" Dave offered.

Dave examined the contents. Multi-coloured, weathered bills held together with string lay scattered on the ground around the case. Apart from three bundles of bills that were stuck together and starting to mold, everything seemed to be in good shape. There were ancient one and two dollar bills bundled together with hundreds. There was even a thousand dollar bill floating on its own.

"This isn't stolen," Dave said decisively. "I think he saved it over a long period of time and took it with him. Maybe he thought he could use it to make a start somewhere. He was a farmer. It was probably his nest egg."

"So why didn't he just put it into an RRSP," asked Don between bites of trail ration.

"My guess is that he was hiding income from the government. Farmers don't always trust the government. Judging from the variety of money here I'd say it took a long time to save this. It might have been Ivy's education fund, or something to augment retirement. It was a one-shot deal."

How ironic that sounded. People only retired these days when they got sick. Education took place mostly through apprenticeship.

A faint breeze lifted the dust. Simultaneously, they looked to the clear horizon.

"Well, let's get back," said Don. "I told Sandy we'd be early."

Chapter 11

One of the Boys

It was already 4:00 when they arrived in Ivy's living room with the heavy case. Jane's note on the table said she would not return until evening. Ivy added her own note to Jane's, saying that she had gone to the play and would be back later, too. They stashed the money behind the couch, for the time being. Then the boys waited in the living room while she freshened up.

This time Ivy looked in the mirror *after* her shower.

"No strawberry curls here," she asserted to her reflection.

A slight breeze moved the white film of curtains on her bedroom window. Now she knew some kind of storm was on its way- sometime. Two breezes in one late-August day had to mean something. From downstairs she could hear laughter muffled by a faint hum. The boys must be play-ing with the burgundy chair. She rustled in her closet for something flattering.

Ivy was always finding new things in her closet. Jane bartered everything from advice to vegetables from her garden. Sometimes people just gave her government rations and things because they were grateful. Today there was no time to try on something new.

Ivy pulled out a powder-blue dress with lemon paisleys that she'd never seen before. It was a light, bamboo-fiber, stretch, mini dress, semi-fitted, with small ruffles down the V, and cap sleeves.

"One size fits all. This will have to do," she said to herself.

Ivy pulled the dress over her head. Then she twisted her hair and clipped it into an up-sweep. She took a moment to examine the effect in the mirror. A satisfied image smiled back at her. In five minutes she had turned herself into an elegant socialite. She pulled on a pair of sandals, leisurely descended the stairs and paused at the living room doorway before making an entrance.

"The switch is on the left arm," Ivy shouted from the door.

Both boys looked up guiltily from the chair they were trying to ride. With mock gallantry, Don strode over and kissed her hand. For the first time Ivy thought she saw some shyness in Dave's fleeting smile. He said only,

"We have the car. Let's go."

As quickly as that they were on their way.

Once at their own house, Don and Dave took a little longer than Ivy to get ready. They came down smelling of shaving lotion and scented soap. She remembered that she'd forgotten to put on perfume.

Now it was Ivy's turn to gape. Both boys wore the same metro-sexual outfits, crisp, dark blue bamboo-fiber pants slung low on the hip with chain mail belts, topped with slim-fitting, cream knit shirts. Dave left the first few buttons of his shirt open. Don's was open almost to the waist and he had added a silver chain around his neck. Dave's disclaimer that dressing alike had more to do with what came down the pike than a fashion statement did not dampen the effect. She had never seen them wear anything but blue jeans.

It felt unreal, but she liked it. Dressed in their finest, Ivy and two very dapper young men piled into the car and sped off to the theater to greet... Sandy.

Sandy looked like a magazine cover girl. Her lipstick matched the peach, silk dress that hugged her perfect body almost to the knees. Silk stockings ended in open-toed stilettos which made her almost as tall as the boys. A few sequins glistened from curls pulled loosely back and cascading down her back. Long, glittering earrings swept across her graceful neck with every movement of her head. She smiled a brilliant smile and held out her hand to Dave, who guided it to Don. Sandy still got them mixed up.

Dave turned to Ivy.

"It's not my turn yet," he said with cool sarcasm.

Ivy looked quizzical, but Dave dismissed it with a wave of his hand.

"I'll explain later."

Sandy chirped something to Don and held his hand in both of hers. He kissed her cheek, glancing sideways at Ivy. Then Sandy turned her brilliance on the others. She beamed at David. She hugged Ivy.

"It looks better on you," Sandy said to Ivy, stepping back to view her at arms-length. "I always liked that dress but it was never 'me', so I gave it up last week. It really suits you, Ivy. I'm glad you got it."

Sandy always said things so nicely.

They were at least a half hour too early for the play. That left time to sit for a while in the park beside the theater. Sandy had brought a crisp, northern apple for each of them- a rare treat these days since apple trees were almost extinct. The exquisite perfume of the apples mingled with Sandy's understated florals. It brought back memories of apple blossoms and bowls of ripe fruit.

Sandy sat close to Don, chirping. Don seemed mesmerized. Dave seemed bored. Ivy was grateful that the burden of small talk did not rest on her. As she lifted the apple to her mouth, she noticed the faint aroma of Sandy's perfume on her hand. Some must have rubbed off during the hug. That meant that she was wearing Sandy's perfume as well as Sandy's dress, and Sandy would leave her perfume all over Don. Ivy turned to face the breeze that was beginning to ripple the fountain. Dave's voice cut through the hum of Sandy's amiable prattle and she turned to face him.

"There are two of us. That makes us 'not third wheels'," he smiled.

Ivy glanced back at Don and Sandy. They did seem to be in their own world. She remembered a light kiss on her ear only that afternoon, and the attraction she and Don had felt for one another out by the stream bed. She called up the image of Don glancing her way to see if she would notice when he kissed Sandy's cheek. She turned back to Dave.

"Why did you think you would have a turn with Sandy?" she asked.

Dave seemed unruffled by the bluntness of her question.

"All the girls like Don. Even you. I can tell," he responded. "And Don likes every girl, until the next one comes

along. He doesn't hurt anyone on purpose. He's just reck-
less, and women love it. He even thinks he's in love with
them. But it always ends when the novelty wears off and
they always pour their hearts out to me."

"And what do they say?" asked Ivy.

Dave knit his brow.

"Oh, the same thing every time. They thought he loved
them until he 'cast them aside'. They can't understand
what happened.

Some of them turn to me next because I look like him.
At first I believed that they were seeing something in me-
that maybe I was more than just their confidante. But
eventually it would become clear that they wanted me to be
Don, and I'm not. I don't even think that Don is the person
they've made him out to be in their minds, the person they
believe they fell in love with. He seems too perfect at first,
too charming."

"Like Sandy," Ivy added.

Don rested his elbows on his knees.

"Yes, like Sandy, and I'd be lying if I said I wasn't at-
tracted to her too. I probably won't take advantage of it
when the time comes, though. It always ends the same way."

"Don't you ever ask anyone out yourself?" she asked.

"I have, but to be honest Don is the charming one. He's
like a chick magnet and I'm the nice guy they want to tell
their life stories to."

"Maybe it's just as well, then, that I'm just one of the
boys," Ivy laughed.

Dave smiled his characteristic dry smile.

"You are *not* just one of the boys," he said.

Chapter 12

Sandy

The wind had picked up by the time the theater let out. Dust from the street stung their legs as they dashed for the shelter of the car. Once inside, Ivy gasped,

"We don't want to be out in what's coming. Let's just get somewhere and wait it out."

Since Sandy was the only one who lived in town, her house was nominated.

It was the longest, shortest trip they had ever taken. Sandy lived only a block away but visibility was sometimes completely obscured by blowing sand and dust. The dash from car to house felt just as treacherous. For once Sandy was speechless.

"Um, can I get you something," she said, as if in shock.

They found themselves in a small drawing room, decorated with an odd mixture of Danish Modern and Victorian furniture. The oddest part was that it had somehow been arranged tastefully. Don threw himself down on the red and navy Chinese rug while Sandy clinked dishes in the kitchen.

Dave and Ivy perched on the couch.

The wind whistled through the eves like a dust blizzard, catching in the crevices of the ledges outside. Ivy lifted an antique phone to call Jane, but the lines were down. She thought about a case full of money stashed behind the couch.

Sandy came in carrying a tray of pears and tea.

"Where do you get all the temperate fruit?" asked Dave.

"There wasn't that much. My aunt brought back 4 apples and 4 pears from a subarctic bio-research lab she was working in last week. She said I could eat one a day, as a treat, until she got back. She left today."

"And where are your parents?" Ivy asked.

Sandy looked away.

"My parents died last year in a tornado in Regina. I've lived with my aunt ever since."

Regaining her composure she pushed the fruit toward her guests.

"This storm could go on for a while. If you really want to share your last pears, maybe we should save them for breakfast," said Ivy. "We've already eaten all your apples."

Suddenly they found themselves in darkness.

"So we have a power outage as well. Must be quite a storm," Ivy added with more irritation than concern.

Don started to speak but Dave stopped him. Wind ripped through the streets with a groan. A muffled sob, hardly audible, mingled with the soft clatter of sand against the window. Ivy pulled a miniature flashlight from her pocket and scanned the room with its beam. The light rested on Sandy, huddled against the wall in terror. She stifled another sob. Like a gallant hero, Don scrambled to

her side and folded her into his arms. The sobbing ceased
with a soft, shuddering breath and all was still. This time
Ivy broke the silence.

"Mind if I turn this off now? I only carry it for emergen-
cies and the battery might not last too long."

Without waiting for a reply she cut the light.

"I take it this is your first sandstorm," said Ivy.

Even Sandy joined in the nervous laughter that followed.

"We can use my little flash to look for some candles and
stuff if you want."

In a clear, firm voice Sandy declined and apologized for
her cowardice. Besides, she didn't know exactly where to
look. She was concerned that the battery would run out
before they found anything.

"Let's just talk!" she added a little too cheerfully.

Ivy peered into the darkness. She imagined Sandy bravely
snuggled into Don's protective arms. So, they would all
be trapped in the dark until the storm ended, listening to
Sandy's social prattle. Sandy continued.

"Why don't we start by taking turns asking each other
questions? We take only one turn each until everyone has
had a chance to ask one question and get a one-sentence
answer. The next time around you can ask two questions,
building on the answer to the first, and so on. The first
question has to relate to the person you are asking. Ivy,
why don't you begin?"

Secretly relieved at being able to get her turn over with
first, Ivy asked,

"OK. What is your aunt doing up north?"

Sandy paused.

"My aunt is growing poison ivy. Now someone has to

ask Ivy something."

Dave cleared his throat uncomfortably. Ivy knew he was thinking of a way to redirect the conversation before Don could jump in, but he was too late.

"Why did they call you poison ivy?" Don asked casually.

"Because I had a bad case of it once and my name is Ivy," she responded, relieved that they would now put it behind them.

Now it was Dave's turn, or Sandy's. Either one of them would know enough to change the subject.

"How did you find out about Ivy's nickname?" Sandy asked Don.

"This isn't fair. I think we should start again and change the subject," Dave protested.

Ivy knew that Don would agree but not for humanitarian reasons. Nobody wanted to end up talking about the money stashed behind Ivy's couch.

"An old family friend told me," Don blurted.

Dave pronounced the game over, but added that he had an impersonal question for Sandy.

"Why would your aunt grow poison ivy when there are food shortages all over the world?"

Sandy actually sounded relieved to be able to explain.

"It's a resilient plant that survives no matter what. If you chop it up into a thousand pieces, each piece from every part of the plant will grow a new one. Scientists have great respect for that plant. Some believe that poison ivy holds the key to adapting vegetation to our changed world."

She paused and then added,

"It's also a better nickname to have in the middle of a sandstorm than 'Sandy'."

Ivy was starting to like that girl.

After that they all sat in the darkness, just talking. They talked until the wind stopped groaning through the streets. They talked until one by one they fell asleep.

Ivy awoke to find herself slumped against Dave on the couch. Don sprawled on the floor, his arm still around sleeping Sandy. Four pears sat, untouched, on a tray left in the middle of the room. A phone was ringing in the next room. They must have fixed the lines.

Ivy struggled to her feet waking Dave, tripped on the rug and stumbled to the phone. It was Jane. Isla would have known from the car-location chip where to find them and told Jane.

"Ivy, there's something behind the living room couch that I think you and your friends will have an explanation for."

Chapter 13

Coming Home

Dave came through the door just as Ivy hung up the phone.

"She found the suitcase," Ivy said.

He seemed unconcerned. At first he said nothing but strode over to Ivy and took both of her hands in his.

"Then we'd better get over there and explain things," he said cheerfully.

Ivy glanced back toward the living room where Don and Sandy lay sleeping in their rumpled evening clothes, unaware that the living-room lights had just blazed on.

"Ivy?" said Dave.

"Yes, we should turn those off," she replied.

She let go of his hands and started to turn away but his hand on her shoulder made her pause.

"That's not what I was going to say and I might not get another chance today."

For the first time since she'd known him Dave seemed to have dropped his mask. His features softened into a warm smile. An uncharacteristic look of uncertainty crossed his face.

"I mean, we spent all that time together in the dark and I never kissed you. I really wanted to."

Ivy's astonished eyes met Dave's. Once again she didn't know whether to feel elated or trapped. Without thinking she slipped her arms around his neck and kissed him, slowly and gently like she'd read about in some of her books. Then Dave touched her cheek and gently brushed back some hair that wasn't in her face in the first place.

"...as long as I'm not 'the bird in the hand'," he said smiling softly.

Ivy let her fingers slide down his arm to rest in his hand. "No more than I am to you."

Now both felt a little uncomfortable so they directed their attention to the situation at hand.

"Let's go wake the sleeping beauties. We still have some explaining to do and I can't have you getting grounded now," said Dave.

"Maybe we should tell Sandy," Ivy added. "We can explain things on the way, if she wants to come."

Don and Sandy were slow to awaken but quickly agreed that everyone should share the adventure. This time Dave drove with Ivy beside him, while the others sat, quiet, in the back listening to Dave's detective version of recent events.

The roads were impassable in places. Work crews labored in the hot sun to clear away the sandy soil, piled up against buildings like concrete snow-drifts.

An hour later, four teens in disheveled evening clothes faced Jane in her living room. A large suitcase of money lay open on the floor between them. Speaking quickly and finishing one anothers' sentences, Ivy and the boys recounted the details of their quest for a treasure that might not even exist.

"...and they didn't want to say anything about Ivy's dad unless the story turned out to be true," Sandy added.

Jane's face relaxed into a look of tired acceptance.

"It's actually good to have closure," she sighed.

Then she looked at Ivy with her best, stern face. She started to speak but her mouth twisted and words caught in her throat. Tears started to form in her eyes and she turned her face away. Sandy and Ivy lunged forward to offer comfort, but both stepped back, surprised.

Jane was stifling a laugh!

"What's so funny!" Ivy exclaimed.

"I guess I'm relieved. Anyway, you all look so guilty, even Sandy, " Jane choked. "Wait! I'll get the camera!"

"No!" they shouted in unison.

"Then I'll fix some brunch."

Sandy followed Jane into the kitchen to help. Don followed Sandy into the kitchen. Ivy and Dave settled back against the couch. There was no need to speak. As Sandy's chatter rippled from the kitchen, Dave smiled a contented smile and took Ivy's hand.

What an intense week it had been. They had weathered two storms. Ivy had lived down her nickname. She had found two good friends and a boyfriend, and it had all started with the worst birthday ever. She felt invincible, joyful, fulfilled.

When the others returned with the food Sandy had already planned their next adventure. It involved going back to her house to explore old boxes in the attic that hadn't been opened in a hundred years.

"That sounds like lots of fun!" Ivy exclaimed.

Jane chuckled,

"First shovel out your room. You left the window open."

Postscript

The environment described in this book is based on recent projections for the Georgian Bay area of Ontario, Canada.